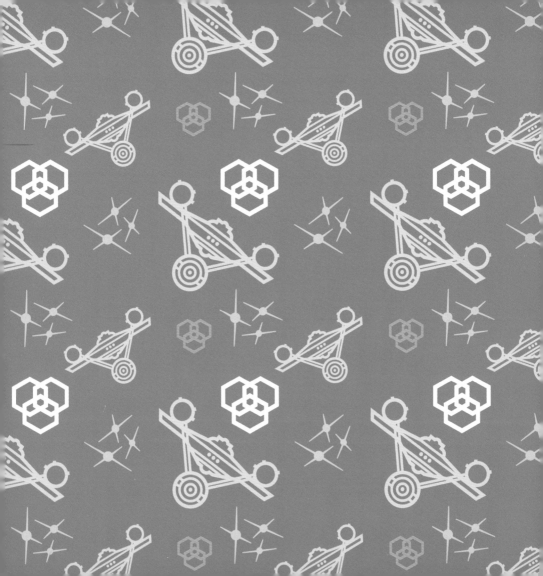

Dedicated to
LEONARD NIMOY

Whose wit and wisdom
made us believe he had been,
and always would be,
our friend.

1931-2015

The Wit and Wisdom of STAR TREK

This is an official licensed edition by Cider Mill Press Book Publishers LLC

13-Digit ISBN: 9781604335644
10-Digit ISBN: 1604335645

This book may be ordered by mail from the publisher. Please include $4.95 for postage and handling.
Please support your local bookseller first!

Books published by Cider Mill Press Book Publishers are available at special discounts for bulk purchases
in the United States by corporations, institutions, and other organizations.
For more information, please contact the publisher.

Cider Mill Press Book Publishers
"Where good books are ready for press"
12 Spring Street
PO Box 454
Kennebunkport, Maine 04046

Visit us on the Web!
www.cidermillpress.com

Design: Alicia Freile, Tango Media
Typography: Alternate Gothic, Industria, and Bank Gothic

Printed in China

1 2 3 4 5 6 7 8 9 0
First Edition

THE
WIT AND WISDOM OF
STAR TREK

Robb Pearlman

CIDER MILL
PRESS

BOOK
PUBLISHERS

Kennebunkport, Maine

INTRODUCTION

STAR TREK, created by Gene Roddenberry, premiered on Thursday, September 8, 1966. Though it aired for only three seasons, it has become a pop culture phenomenon loved by millions of fans around the world. It spawned an animated series, four live action series, a thriving motion picture franchise, video games, hundreds of books and comic books. Packed with action, adventure, and accurate predictions of now-commonplace technology, the series is hailed for the clever and creative ways it examines social and political issues. By placing the men and women of the future (along with some aliens) in situations like those faced by viewers, the wit and wisdom imbued into each episode of STAR TREK continues to provide generations with smart, compassionate, and inspirational ways to live as boldly as any Starfleet officer.

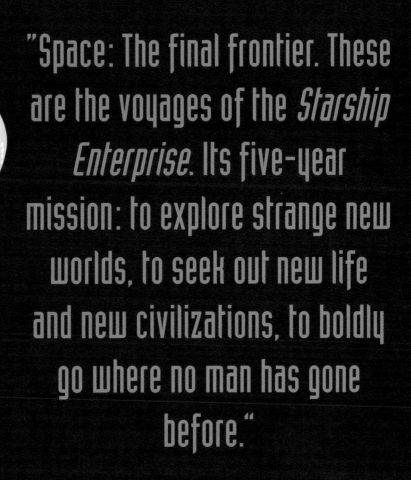

"Space: The final frontier. These are the voyages of the *Starship Enterprise*. Its five-year mission: to explore strange new worlds, to seek out new life and new civilizations, to boldly go where no man has gone before."

"**ONE DAY SOON**, man is going to be able to harness incredible energies—maybe even the atom—energies that could ultimately hurl us to other worlds in some sort of spaceship. And the men that reach out into space will be able to find ways to feed the hungry millions of the world and to cure their diseases. They will be able to find a way to give each man hope and a common future... and those are the days worth living for."

EDITH KEELER, "THE CITY ON THE EDGE OF FOREVER"

"Only a fool would stand in the way of progress."

KIRK, "THE ULTIMATE COMPUTER"

"Change is the essential process of all existence."

SPOCK, "LET THAT BE YOUR LAST BATTLEFIELD"

"He's dead, Jim."

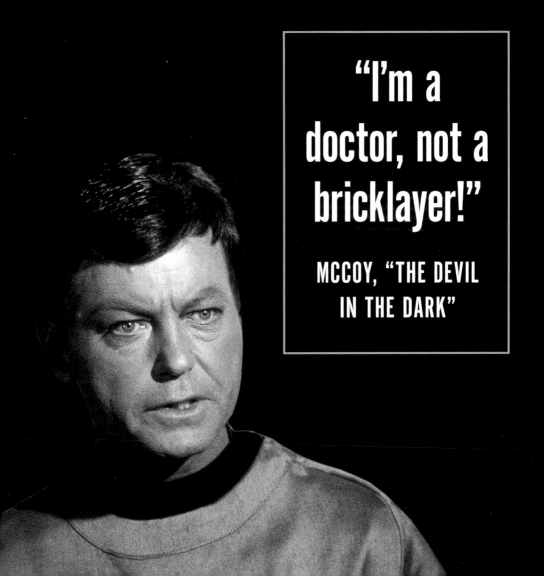

"I'm a doctor, not a bricklayer!"

MCCOY, "THE DEVIL IN THE DARK"

"DEATH, DESTRUCTION, DISEASE, HORROR.

That's what war is all about... That's what makes it a thing to be avoided."

KIRK, "A TASTE OF ARMAGEDDON"

"WITHOUT FOLLOWERS, EVIL CANNOT SPREAD."

SPOCK, "AND THE CHILDREN SHALL LEAD"

"Khan is my name."
"Khan, nothing more?"
"Khan."

KHAN AND KIRK, "SPACE SEED"

"You see, in our century, we've learned not to fear words."

UHURA,
"THE SAVAGE CURTAIN"

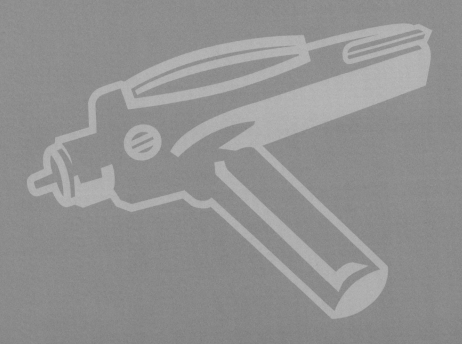

"WAR IS NEVER IMPERATIVE..."

McCoy, "Balance of Power"

"LIBERTY AND FREEDOM have to be more than just words."

KIRK, "THE OMEGA GLORY"

"I think children have an instinctive need for adults; they want to be told right and wrong."

KIRK, "MIRI"

LEONARD NIMOY WAS, IN REALITY, ONLY SEVEN YEARS YOUNGER THAN MARK LENARD, WHO PORTRAYED HIS FATHER, SAREK.

"SCOTTY, BEAM US UP!"

"Scotty is 99% James Doohan and 1% accent."

JAMES DOOHAN

"There's an old saying on Earth, Mister Sulu. Fool me once, shame on you. Fool me twice, shame on me."
"I KNOW THIS SAYING. IT WAS INVENTED IN RUSSIA."

KIRK AND CHEKOV, "FRIDAY'S CHILD"

"HIS BRAIN IS GONE!"

MCCOY,
"SPOCK'S BRAIN"

"You try to cross brains with Spock, he'll cut you to pieces every time."

SULU, "THE CORBOMITE MANEUVER"

"You pointy-eared hobgoblin!"

MCCOY, "BREAD AND CIRCUSES"

"MAN STAGNATES IF
HE HAS NO AMBITION,
NO DESIRE TO BE MORE
THAN HE IS."

KIRK, "THIS SIDE OF PARADISE"

"There are certain absolutes, Mr. Spock, and one of them is the right of humanoids to a free and unchained environment; the right to have conditions that permit growth."

MCCOY, "THE APPLE"

"Too much of anything, Lieutenant, even love, isn't necessarily a good thing."

KIRK, "THE TROUBLE WITH TRIBBLES"

"AFTER A TIME, YOU MAY
FIND THAT HAVING IS NOT SO
PLEASING A THING AFTER ALL
AS WANTING. IT IS NOT LOGICAL,
BUT IT IS OFTEN TRUE."

SPOCK, "AMOK TIME"

"The heart is not a **LOGICAL ORGAN.**"

DOCTOR JANET WALLACE, "THE DEADLY YEARS"

"One man cannot summon the future."

"BUT ONE MAN CAN CHANGE THE PRESENT."

MIRROR SPOCK AND KIRK, "MIRROR MIRROR"

"Kirk to Enterprise..."

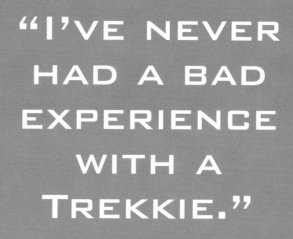

"I'VE NEVER HAD A BAD EXPERIENCE WITH A TREKKIE."

GENE RODDENBERRY

"Hailing frequencies open."

Nichelle Nichols' performance as Lieutenant Uhura proved to be so popular and empowering that she was contracted by NASA to recruit women and minorities into the space program.

"CAPTAIN'S LOG..."

"I always use a stunt double.
Except in love scenes. I insist on
doing those myself."

WILLIAM SHATNER

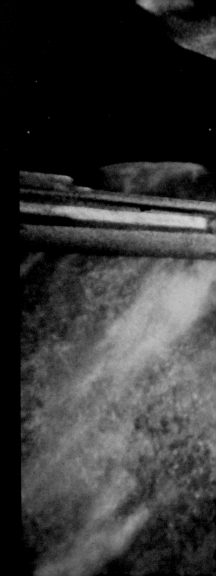

"May we never find space so vast, planets so cold, heart and mind so empty that, that we cannot fill them with **LOVE AND WARMTH.**"

DOCTOR TRISTAN ADAMS,
"DAGGER OF THE MIND"

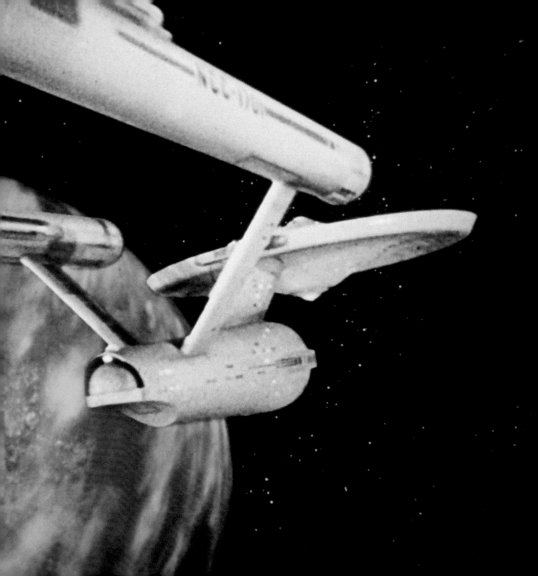

"We're all sorry for the other guy when he loses his job to a machine. When it comes to your job, that's different. And it will always be different."

MCCOY, "THE ULTIMATE COMPUTER"

"I SPEAK OF RIGHTS. A MACHINE HAS NONE. A MAN MUST!"

SAMUEL T. COGLEY, "COURT MARTIAL"

"When *Star Trek* was canceled after its second season, it was the activism of the fans that revived it for a third season."

GEORGE TAKEI

"Nobody helps nobody but himself."

OXMYX, "A PIECE OF THE ACTION"

"CAPTAIN, YOU'RE AN EXCELLENT STARSHIP COMMANDER. BUT AS A TAXI DRIVER, YOU LEAVE MUCH TO BE DESIRED."

SPOCK, "A PIECE OF THE ACTION"

"Are you trying to be funny, Mister Spock?" "It would never occur to me, Captain."

KIRK AND SPOCK,
"THE IMMUNITY SYNDROME"

"I object to intellect without discipline. I object to power without constructive purpose."

SPOCK, "THE SQUIRE OF GOTHOS"

"WITHOUT FREEDOM OF CHOICE
THERE IS NO CREATIVITY.
WITHOUT CREATIVITY,
THERE IS NO LIFE."

KIRK, "THE RETURN OF THE ARCHONS"

"HOPE? I always thought that was a Human failing, Mr. Spock."

"TRUE, DOCTOR. CONSTANT EXPOSURE DOES RESULT IN A CERTAIN DEGREE OF CONTAMINATION."

MCCOY AND SPOCK,
"THE GAMESTERS OF TRISKELION"

"MR. SPOCK, you're the most cold-blooded man I've ever known."

"WHY, THANK YOU, DOCTOR."

MCCOY AND SPOCK, "COURT MARTIAL"

The name "Uhura" comes from the Swahili word for freedom.

Though an integral part of the crew and legacy of STAR TREK, Walter Koenig's Chekov didn't appear until the series' second season.

"Fascinating."

"Mr. Scott, there are always alternatives."

SPOCK, "THE GALILEO SEVEN"

"THIS TROUBLED PLANET IS A PLACE OF THE MOST VIOLENT CONTRASTS. THOSE WHO RECEIVE THE REWARDS ARE TOTALLY SEPARATED FROM THOSE WHO SHOULDER THE BURDENS. IT IS NOT A WISE LEADERSHIP."

SPOCK, "THE CLOUD MINDERS"

"ONE OF THE ADVANTAGES of being a captain, doctor, is being able to ask for advice without necessarily having to take it."

KIRK, "DAGGER OF THE MIND"

"We're a most promising species, Mister Spock, as predators go."

KIRK, "ARENA"

THE SCENES IN WHICH KIRK AND THE GORN FIGHT IN "ARENA" WERE FILMED ON LOCATION AT CALIFORNIA'S VASQUEZ ROCKS.

"EATING
is a
pleasure."

KIRK,
"WHAT ARE LITTLE
GIRLS MADE OF?"

"Where I come from, size, shape or color makes no difference."

KIRK, "PLATO'S STEPCHILDREN"

"I HAVE NOTED THAT THE HEALTHY RELEASE OF EMOTION IS FREQUENTLY VERY UNHEALTHY FOR THOSE CLOSEST TO YOU."

SPOCK, "PLATO'S STEPCHILDREN"

"Leave any bigotry in your quarters. There's no room for it on the bridge."

KIRK, "BALANCE OF TERROR"

The scenes in which the Enterprise *was being attacked were filmed by shaking the cameras as the actors flung themselves across the set of the bridge.*

"The glory of creation is
in its infinite diversity."
"And the ways our
differences combine to create
meaning and beauty."

MIRANDA AND SPOCK,
"IS THERE IN TRUTH NO BEAUTY?"

"A LOT CAN HAPPEN IN A YEAR. PLEASE, GIVE YOURSELF EVERY MINUTE."

STAR TREK *entered syndication in the autumn of 1969, less than a year after the series' final new episode aired.*

MAJEL BARRETT *is sometimes called "The First Lady of* STAR TREK.*" Not only was she married to creator Gene Rodenberry, she portrayed "Number One" in the original pilot episode of* STAR TREK, *Christine Chapel in* STAR TREK, STAR TREK: The Motion Picture *and* STAR TREK IV: The Voyage Home, *several voice roles on* STAR TREK: The Animated Series, *Lwaxana Troi and the voice of the computer on* STAR TREK: The Next Generation, STAR TREK: Deep Space Nine, STAR TREK: Voyager, *as well as the series' films, and video games.*

"Energize!"

> # "A ROOM SHOULD REFLECT ITS OCCUPANT."
>
> ## KIRK, "WINK OF AN EYE"

Jefferies Tubes, the shafts in which Scotty often made necessary repairs (and the hiding place of Ambassador Gav's body) were named after production designer Matt Jefferies.

STAR TREK's original pilot, "The Cage," was never broadcast. With the exception of Spock, it featured an entirely different crew on the Enterprise (and according to canon, took place before Captain Kirk took the helm). Scenes from that episode were repurposed and used in season one's two-part "The Menagerie, Part I" episodes.

"Beep."

PIKE,
"THE MENAGERIE, PART I"

STAR TREK *was produced by Desilu, the company founded by* I Love Lucy *stars Lucille Ball and Desi Arnaz.*

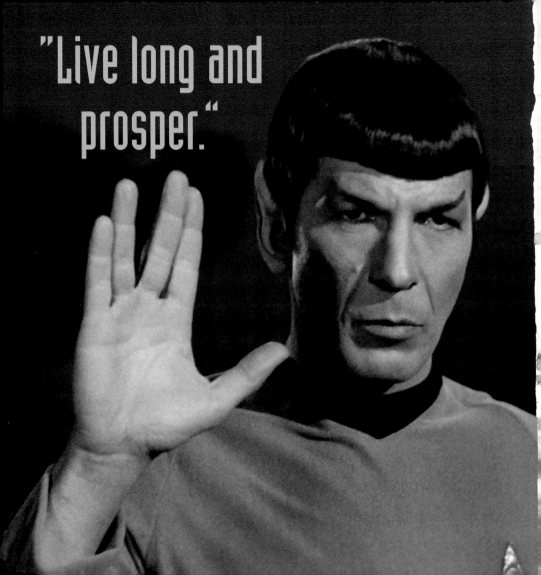
"Live long and prosper."